MySELF Bookshelf

Mommy and Daddy Love You

By Cecil Kim

Illustrated by Anna Ladecka

Language Arts Consultant: Joy Cowley

NORWOOD HOUSE PRESS

Chicago, Illinois

DEAR CAREGIVER

MySELF Bookshelf is a series of books that support children's social emotional learning. SEL has been proven to promote not only the development of self-awareness, responsibility, and positive relationships, but also academic achievement.

Current research reveals that the part of the brain that manages emotion is directly connected to the part of the brain that is used in cognitive tasks, such as: problem solving, logic, reasoning, and critical thinking—all of which are at the heart of learning.

SEL is also directly linked to what are referred to as 21st Century Skills: collaboration, communication, creativity, and critical thinking. MySELF Bookshelf offers an early start that will help children build the competencies for success in school and life.

In these delightful books, young children practice early reading skills while learning how to manage their own feelings and how to be considerate of other perspectives. Each book focuses on aspects of SEL that help children develop social competence that will benefit them in their relationships with others as well as in their school success. The charming characters in the stories model positive traits such as: responsibility, goal setting, determination, patience, and celebrating differences. At the end of each story, you will find a letter that highlights the positive traits and an activity or discussion to help your child apply SEL to his or her own life.

Above all, the most important part of the reading experience is to have fun and enjoy it!

Sincerely,

Shannon Cannon

Shannon Cannon, Ph.D.
Literacy and SEL Consultant

Norwood House Press • P.O. Box 316598 • Chicago, Illinois 60631
For more information about Norwood House Press please visit our website at www.norwoodhousepress.com or call 866-565-2900.

Shannon Cannon – Literacy and SEL Consultant
Joy Cowley – English Language Arts Consultant
Mary Lindeen – Consulting Editor

Library of Congress Cataloging-in-Publication Data
    Kim, Cecil.
    Mommy and Daddy love you / by Cecil Kim ; illustrated By Anna Ladecka.
        pages cm. -- (MySelf bookshelf)
    Summary: "When Nina hears the news that her parents are getting a divorce, she is scared, angry, and sad. Why is this happening? Nina becomes very mad and acts badly. After some adjusting, Nina begins to understand the situation and that Mommy and Daddy will always love her"-- Provided by publisher.
    ISBN 978-1-59953-656-9 (library edition : alk. paper) -- ISBN 978-1-60357-716-8 (ebook)
    [1. Divorce--Fiction. 2. Parent and child--Fiction.] I. Ladecka, Anna, illustrator. II. Title.
    PZ7.K55958Mo 2015
    [E]--dc23
                            2014030339

Manufactured in the United States of America in Stevens Point, Wisconsin.
263N—122014

Nina heard some terrible news.
It was the worst thing
she had ever heard
in her entire life.
Mommy and Daddy
were getting a divorce.

Nina felt as scared as a rabbit.

Her parents were splitting up.

She was going to stay with Mommy.

Daddy would live in another house.

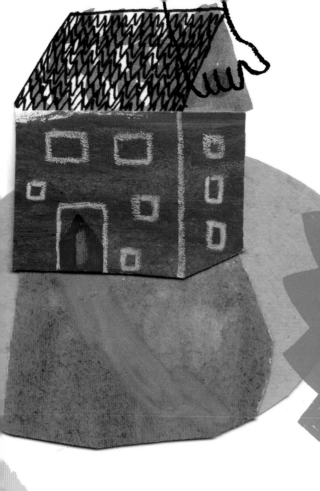

Nina begged like a puppy. "Mommy, I'll be a good girl. Daddy. I'll study harder."

Mommy said, "Nina, darling, we are not splitting up because of you."

Daddy said, "It is because Mommy and I have decided we will be happier living apart than living together."

That night, Nina felt gloomy.
She felt like a bat in a dark cave.
So many worries filled her mind
she could not sleep.

The next day, Daddy was packing.
Nina was like a naughty monkey.
She took Daddy's things and hid them.
Then she pretended her finger hurt.

13

14

Daddy said, "Nina, you and I will get to spend time together on Saturdays. We'll eat yummy food, and maybe we'll even go on a trip somewhere."

Nina didn't answer.

As Daddy left, he said, "I will always love you, Nina."

Nina felt spiky like a porcupine. "Lies!" she said. "All grown-ups are liars!"

Nina got very angry.

She hated her house.

She hated her mommy.

She hated her homework.

She wouldn't eat.

She felt like an angry gorilla.

Then Nina saw her mother crying.
Mommy didn't make a sound.
Her shoulders shook
and tears ran down her face.
Nina could not go to her.

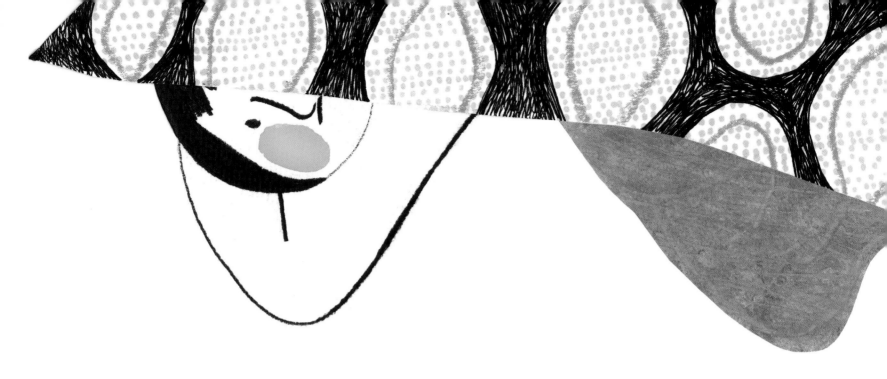

After that, Nina did not get angry.
She did not laugh.
She did not even talk.
She was like a turtle
in a hard shell.

Nina's teacher said to her,
"Nina, your mother told me
about the changes in your family.
I am so sorry. This must be
a hard time for you. It's okay
if you feel upset or sad. I understand."
Nina's teacher gave her a hug,
and Nina began to cry.
She opened her mouth like a hippo
and cried and cried.

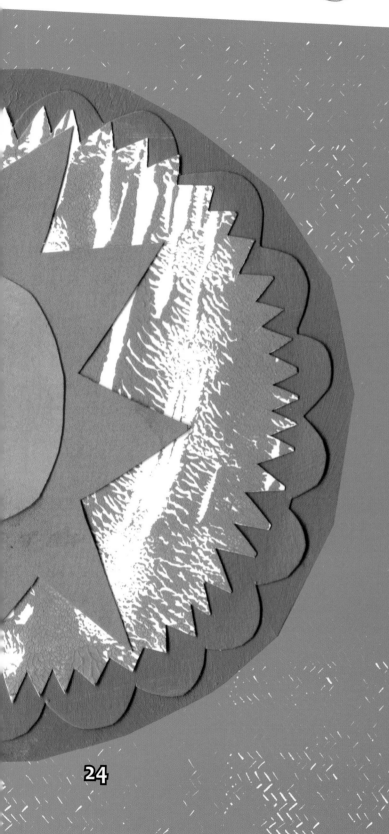

When Nina got home,
she gave her mommy a hug.
Nina was like a cuddly bear.
She said, "It's okay, Mommy."

Mommy said, "Yes, Nina.
We're going to be okay."

At last it was Saturday.

Nina was very happy to see Daddy.

They went to the zoo together.

She held his hand tightly.

She had been to the zoo before

with Mommy and Daddy.

Now it was just Daddy

and that was okay.

She still had her mom and dad.

Their love for her had not changed.

Dearest Nina,

Daddy and Mommy are both very sorry that you are feeling so sad. We want you to know that we both tried our best to keep our family together. We did everything we could think of to find a way to stay together and be happy. But nothing worked. So we decided that living apart from each other was the best choice for us. It was a hard decision to make, because we knew how much it would change your life. We love you so much that we did not want to make you feel pain or sadness.

We hope that as time goes by, the pain and sadness will heal for all of us. We know that all of these changes in our family will feel different at first, and it's okay to feel sad about that. Every new thing in life feels different at first. We believe that after awhile these changes will start to feel normal and that we will all be okay. We also know one thing that will never ever change—our love for you!

With love from Mommy and Daddy

SOCIAL AND EMOTIONAL LEARNING FOCUS

Emotions

When Nina learned that her parents were getting a divorce, she had many feelings. The author of the story sometimes uses similes to describe those feelings. A simile is a comparison of two things using the words like or as. For example, "She was like a turtle in a hard shell." When you are aware of your feelings, you are better able to manage them to help you feel better.

Think of four feelings you might have. Write a list. Then, you can make a **Feelings Flap Book** to describe your feelings using similes and pictures to describe them.

- Fold a piece of 8 ½ x 11 inch paper vertically (hotdog fold).

- Fold it horizontally 2 times to make 8 sections.

- Unfold the paper and cut on the short folds on the left side toward the middle (only cut half way).

- Fold vertically again, as in the first step.

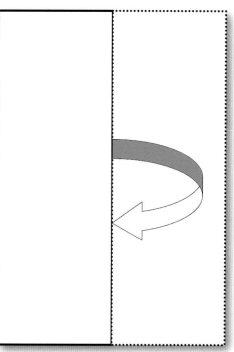

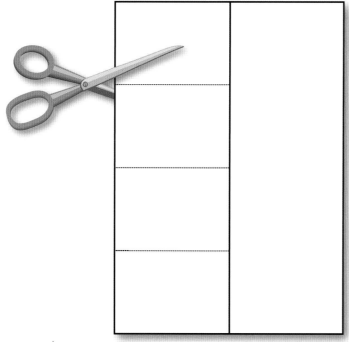

(continued on next page)

- Write each of the feelings on the outside.

- On the inside, write each of the similes on the left and draw a picture on the right.

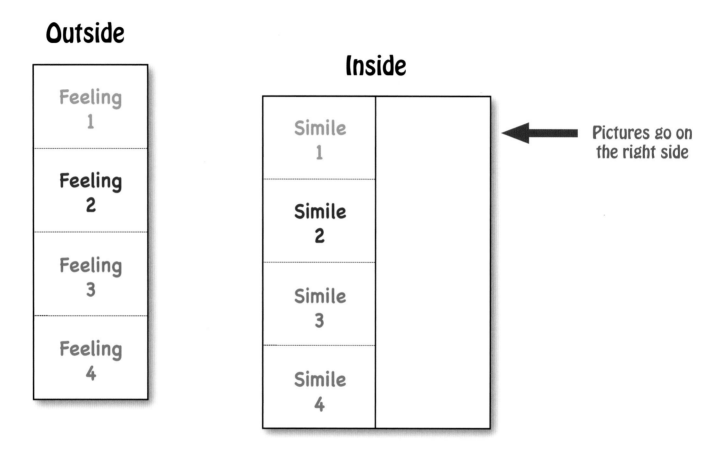

Outside

Feeling 1
Feeling 2
Feeling 3
Feeling 4

Inside

Simile 1	
Simile 2	
Simile 3	
Simile 4	

← Pictures go on the right side

Reader's Theater

Reader's Theater is an interactive approach to reading that allows students to understand each story through dramatic interpretation. By involving students in reading, listening, and speaking activities, they provide an integrated approach for students to develop fluency and comprehension. A Reader's Theater edition of this book is available online. You can access the script by scanning the QR code to the right or visit our website at:
http://www.norwoodhousepress.com/mommyanddaddy.aspx